Baby
Tugs Bear

Care Bears, Young World of Care Bears, Tenderheart Bear, Friend Bear, Grumpy Bear, Birthday Bear, Cheer Bear, Funshine Bear, Love-a-Lot Bear, Wish Bear, Good Luck Bear, Baby Hugs Bear, and Baby Tugs Bear are trademarks of American Greetings Corporation.

Library of Congress Cataloging in Publication Data: Mason, Evelyn. The baby hugs bear and baby tugs bear look and find book. (Young world of Care Bears) SUMMARY: Baby Tugs Bear and Baby Hugs Bear try to find a fallen star with help from the reader.
1. Children's stories, American. 2. Toy and movable books — Specimens.
[1. Bears — Fiction.   2.   Stars — Fiction.   3.   Toy and movable books]
I.   Cooke, Tom, ill.   II.   Title.   III.   Series.
PZ7.M388Bab   1984   [E]   84-14905   ISBN 0-910313-73-3
Manufactured in the United States of America   2 3 4 5 6 7 8 9 0   -01

The Care Bears

The Baby Hugs Bear and Baby Tugs Bear
Look and Find Book

Story by Evelyn Mason
Pictures by Tom Cooke

In the land of Care-a-Lot Baby Hugs Bear
and Baby Tugs Bear were busy playing ball.
"Can you catch a fly ball?" asked Baby Tugs.
"I can catch it," answered Baby Hugs. She
put her hands high in the air and pulled the
ball toward her tummy.

"Good catch!" Grams Bear said.
"Will you play catch with us, Grams?"
asked Baby Tugs Bear and Baby Hugs Bear.
"Sure I will," said Grams, who always
liked playing ball.

After she had played for a few minutes,
Grams left Baby Tugs and Baby Hugs to play
by themselves. "Don't run too near the edge
of a cloud," she warned as she walked away.

When Baby Hugs Bear and Baby Tugs Bear
got tired of playing, they sat down to rest.

From their seats in Care-a-Lot, Baby Hugs
Bear and Baby Tugs Bear counted stars. "One,
two, three, four, five, six, seven, eight...I see
eight stars," said Baby Hugs.

"Let me count, too," said Baby Tugs.

"One, two, three, four, five, six , seven…"
Before Baby Tugs could finish counting, one
of the stars fell from where it was twinkling
and shot across the sky.

"Where does a star go when it falls?"
asked Baby Hugs Bear.
"I don't know," answered Baby Tugs Bear.
"Let's ask Grams."

Baby Hugs Bear and Baby Tugs Bear found Grams Bear.

"Where does a star go when it falls?" they asked.

"Falling stars go to the earth below us — you know that," Grams said.

"But exactly where do they land?"

"Hop in my Cloud Car and let's find out,"
answered Grams.

"This is an adventure," Baby Tugs said.
"It's a find-a-falling-star adventure."

ZOOM! Grams was a good driver and her Cloud Car sped to earth.

Grams pulled up in front of a bakery and
said, "The two of you can start looking for the
star right here on this street. I'll keep my eye
on you, and we'll meet in an hour. Don't look
for trouble; just look for the star."

"Star, where are you?" asked Baby
Hugs Bear.

"I see a star," said Baby Tugs. "Do you see one, too?"

"I see it," answered Baby Hugs, "but it's not *our* star!"

Where is the star that Baby Tugs Bear sees?

"Star, where are you?" Baby Hugs Bear
asked again.

"I see a star," said Baby Tugs Bear. "Do
you see one, too?"

"I see it," answered Baby Hugs, "but it's
not *our* star!"

Where is the star that Baby Hugs Bear sees?

Baby Hugs Bear and Baby Tugs Bear
walked down the street until they came to a
school. They shouted together, "Star, where
are you?"

A small boy heard their shouting and said,
"If you look through the window, I think
you'll find a star."

"But that's not *our* star," said Baby Hugs and
Baby Tugs to the boy who tried to help them.

Baby Hugs Bear and Baby Tugs Bear
ran towards the playground. This time Baby
Tugs was the first one to shout, "Star, where
are you?"

There was no answer.
*There is a star on the playground, but it's hard
to see. Can you find it?*

Baby Hugs Bear and Baby Tugs Bear sat down to think.

"Where should we go?" asked Baby Hugs Bear.

Baby Tugs Bear answered, "I saw a sign in town. It said: CIRCUS TODAY AT THE FAIRGROUND. Let's look for our star at the circus."

"Will Grams Bear know where to find us?"
"Before we leave, we'll tell her where we are going," said Baby Tugs.

The Baby Care Bears ran as fast as they could. They told Grams Bear that they were sure they would find their star at the circus. She gave them permission to go.

Before they went into the circus tent they
stopped to watch the parade.
Can you point to all the stars in the parade?

Inside the circus tent there were star-spangled elephants and star-spangled riders.

There were big stars and little stars; high stars and low stars.

But Baby Hugs Bear and Baby Tugs Bear
could still not find their star.
Can you find their star?
Finally they stopped to talk to a clown.
"Have you seen our star?" they asked.
The clown did not speak, but he pointed
Baby Hugs and Baby Tugs in the right direction.

There in the center ring Baby Hugs and
Baby Tugs found their star!

Baby Tugs Bear shouted, "Star, we found you!"

"That's our star!" Baby Hugs Bear exclaimed.
The seal gave them a playful wink and
tossed their star to Baby Hugs.
Both Baby Care Bears smiled at each other.
Then Baby Tugs Bear saw Grams Bear
coming toward them.

"I've been keeping an eye on you,"
Grams said. "I knew you'd find your star and
you did."

Baby Hugs Bear and Baby Tugs Bear
showed Grams the star, then they all hopped
into her Cloud Car.

Baby Hugs wanted to hold the star all the way home. But Baby Tugs wanted to hold it too.

Grams said, "Baby Hugs, you can hold it first. I'll tell you when we're half-way home, so you can give it to your brother."

Can you find all the stars that the Care Bears passed on the way home?

As soon as the Cloud Car stopped in the
land of Care-a-Lot, Baby Hugs Bear said,
"I want to hang the star right now!"

"But I want to hang it," said Baby
Tugs Bear.

Grams Bear said, "You can do it together."

And that's just what they did.